Anika & Edward

"Anika & Edward," by Stefan Scheuermann. ISBN 978-1-63868-058-1 (softcover); 978-1-63868-059-8 (hardcover)

Published 2022 by Virtualbookworm.com Publishing Inc., P.O. Box 9949, College Station, TX 77842, US.

Part One:

The Cats' Alley

Like most births, Anika's entry into the world was anticipated with joy and hope. There were three in the intimate circle of excitement. Anika's parents, Mary and Fergus, lived on the farm with Mary's mother. It was a small family farm, northeast of Dundee, Scotland, which had been acquired by one of Mary's ancestors long forgotten. The three of them worked the farm, and their six hands were all that the farm needed — until Anika's first breath of earthly air.

That first breath coincided with Mary's last. The mother's life was exchanged for the child's. With the loss of Mary, and the widowed Fergus occupied with a baby, the farm's six hands became two, and other arrangements needed to be made. The farm was no longer the place for Fergus or his new daughter, and the grandmother needed more help than Fergus could give.

Fergus' ambitions for Anika's future spurred him into change. With the grandmother's support and insistence, he went to Edinburgh with infant Anika to complete his education. Along with his daughter and his eternal devotion to his dead wife, Fergus had one great passion, one he shared with his mother-in-law. He loved Scottish literature, and had wiled many a late hour with dramatic readings in the farmhouse. When Anika's grandmother kissed them both goodbye, she expressed only one regret to Fergus— that their late-night readings would be on indefinite hold.

Fergus took quite naturally back to the halls of academia. Oh, he was quite in his element. He had met Mary in school, and upon his return to a college campus, he was often heard speaking out loud to her, as if she still strode the halls beside him. Anika? Well, she was an infant, and the university quickly became all that she knew. They lived on the campus, Fergus and Anika together. He studied aloud, and she was steeped early in the heavy scribblings of Carmichael and Hume, and the prancing couplets of Robert Burns and Walter Scott. Fergus read it all with silly faces and fluctuating voices to entertain his daughter while he studied, and Anika giggled equally at it all.

The university was a city within itself. Fergus was at home there and found no reason to leave. He called his mother-in-law. He wrote to his mother-in-law. But he never left the campus. Anika's first steps were in the university halls. Her first words were to students and professors. Her first teeth chewed the meals from a campus cafeteria.

Now, it was not a common practice for the university to hire its own graduates. If ever an exception was to be made, it was in the case of Fergus. Before he graduated, he found himself more often in fiery debate with professors than with his fellow students. His transition from student to faculty was seamless. His passion and charisma was aided by the bright and adorable toddler always at his side.

It was not long before Anika began venturing her own opinions in the rousing, animated symposiums that seemed to follow her father around like a hungry puppy. But Carmichael and Hume were not nearly fanciful enough for her wild mind. She much preferred the colorful imagery of the poets. During readings and debates on Enlightenment philosophers, her comments always turned to the fantastical, and the conversations left her behind like a freight train too fast to jump. It never saddened her long. She took the tasty tidbits of quips and phrases being flung around her and stirred them into a whimsical stew for her own consumption. Oh the adventures she went on, the creatures she rode upon, all while sitting still in a chair at her father's side, or sitting on his feet under a table.

In what seemed a moment to Fergus, Anika no longer fit under the table. She no longer toddled at his side. She loved her father dearly. He was the only family she ever knew. But each door at the university enticed her and she began to explore. Every door opened to the lovely child, and Anika absorbed lectures and debates in a broad variety of subjects.

Within the university was a primary school. When Anika turned five, she attended during the day. In the afternoons, the university campus was hers. In the evenings, she had her father. That is where she bloomed. Fergus still read to her as he always had, still making the same silly faces and fluctuating voices, and still receiving the giggles in response. Added to the readings were Anika's own recitations — dramatic renditions of the adventures that were spawned, developed, and played out in full vigor within her mind, each bearing a hint of flavor from her many university influences. They were every bit as animated as Fergus' readings, and they received in response an equally hearty giggle.

Anika made friends in her school. That is to say, she played with other children. But they were quickly from her thoughts after being dismissed from her classroom. Awaiting her were friends much more familiar — the stone steps of the old campus buildings, the dark oak wainscoting, the marble busts of long-dead scholars, and there at the end of them all waited always her dear father. That is, until Anika was twelve years old.

That fateful evening, she waited in her room for Fergus. He was later than usual, so her excitement was all the more abundant when she heard the outer door open.

"Anika?" called out a distantly familiar voice.

Anika turned the corner to see not her father, but a tall, chisel-chinned, but kindly looking gentleman with reddened, dewy eyes and an expression of anguished compassion on his face. She had seen him before. She had heard him before. But her panicked mind could not reach for such details.

"Where is my father?" she asked in a hurried voice.

The gentleman explained in the calmest and gentlest terms possible that her father passed away. She did not hear when. She did not hear how. Perhaps these things were explained, but she would not have known. She collapsed above her buckling knees and struck her head on the floor. The ceiling above her spun, then turned a hazy brown, then disappeared entirely into darkness.

Anika awoke in the night, in her own bed. The kind gentleman slept on a chair beside her. She cried as silently as she could, trying not to wake the bearer of such horrible news, afraid that if he awoke, he would speak again and confirm the tragedy. She bit on the inside of her lips and crept from her bed. As she cut each corner, as she breached each threshold, she half-expected to see her father. But Fergus was gone, gone from the rooms, from the university, from Anika's life, and from the world. Anika crawled into her father's bed, planted her face in the pillow, and allowed the rush of the familiar smell to cradle her back to sleep.

In the morning, there was a bustle outside of Fergus' room. Anika emerged and was greeted covetously by the kind gentleman.

"It is best that you...," he began, "That is to say, we have agreed that you should be taken immediately to your family."

"What family?" Anika inquired honestly, "I have no family."

"Of course you have family. Your grandmother awaits you on the farm where you were born. You should be with her now and somebody will take you there immediately."

Losing her father, Anika felt like the entire world disappeared before her eyes. But how much more would she lose? She looked around at the walls and the furniture, at the window seat where her father used to read to her, at the bench against the wall where she would stand and recite her fantastic tales. In her father's death, those things were all that were left to her, all that connected her to him. She had no memory of the farm. It was a strange place to her, and her grandmother a stranger. Her things were packed by faceless hands and she was whisked from the rooms she had shared with her father since her infancy, and torn from the last remaining connection to him.

She was seated on a bench in the vestibule, too angry to cry and too nervous to protest. It had all happened so quickly, and she could not place her thoughts in order. She was greeted by a small, wiry, balding, graying man, whose shoulders were too narrow for his head. He was carrying Fergus' trunk, packed with Anika's things.

"A-A-Anika," the nervous little man stuttered, "I am to take you to your grandmother's. C-C-Come, m-my car is waiting in front."

At the thought of leaving the university, she was struck by a panicked sense of loss. Not only was her father's life taken from her, but her own life was being taken as well, the only life she had ever known, to be replaced by one that existed only in the hazy, half-forgotten tales her father used to tell of her infancy.

She gathered the wits and the courage to announce, "I don't want to stay with my grandmother. I don't remember her. I want to stay here, at the university."

"Nonsense," responded the little man with a boldness that seemed to come from some other person's mouth, "You can't live at the university!"

"But I have always lived here. This is my home."

"N-N-Not always," he returned with his usual meek stutter, "I was told to take you to your grandmother's, where you lived before your father came here."

Anika was alone, with nobody to fight her case. She determined to go to her grandmother's and be so unbearably contrary and irksome that her grandmother would call the university within two days and demand that they take her back. So she followed the little man to his car. He was a weak man, as slight of figure as a full-grown man can be, but his car was so tiny that he looked quite substantial beside it. The trunk barely squeezed through the door and into the back seat, and needed every bit of the faint encouragement the weak little man could give it. But it finally boarded and so did the driver. He lifted his bony knees to nearly touch his pointed chin as he mounted the driver's side.

He closed the door with a creak and a thwack, then rolled the dirty driver's side window down one quarter of the way. He tried to lower it farther, but the old window on the much older car had not gone lower in many years. He banged on the window and tried again, as he had countless times before, with equal fruitlessness. He finally gave up and gestured to Anika, instructing her with a wave of his hand to walk around to the passenger side.

Content with her plan, Anika obeyed, but when she reached the other side and opened the door, and saw how snugly she would be situated against her chauffeur, she squeezed behind her designated seat to sit in the back. She was pressed all the more tightly against the trunk, but it was her father's trunk. The man sighed, clearly insulted. He shrugged his shoulders, said, "Have it your way," started the car, and drove away from the only home Anika could remember.

Anika did not pay attention to each turn and each building, but even in her absent-mindedness, she knew they were driving in circles. They must have been driving for twenty minutes, but they had not left the university.

"Do you know how to get to my grandmother's?" Anika asked timidly.

"Uh-uh, of course I can get you there," he answered defensively, "if I can find my way out of Edinburgh."

"Out of Edinburgh?" she returned, "You have not yet taken us off the campus."

"Y-Y-Yes, w-w-well, I have not left the campus in eight years."

"EIGHT YEARS?!" she shouted at a volume suited to a much larger environment, "You live at the university?"

"W-W-Well, yes."

"But I thought you can't live at the university."

"That's not what I said," he replied with uncharacteristic confidence, "I said that *you* could not live at the university."

"So why can you?"

"Because I work there, and you do not."

"I could work there too," she suggested, beginning to abandon her plan in favor of an immediate return to her room.

"And what would *you* do?" he asked with extreme condescension in his voice.

"I could teach literature, like my father."

"Oh yes, little one," he came back snidely, "Professor Anika's Medieval Scottish Poetry Course, sign me up!"

With rich sorrow in her faltering voice, Anika rebutted, "My father did not teach *medieval* poetry."

Her driver, never a notably compassionate man, was hit by the impropriety of his comment. He had been arguing heartlessly with a young orphan in the throes of grief. He stuttered the beginnings of an apology, but he could not seem to successfully glue two syllables together. Anika folded her arms, lowered her eyes, and began plotting her first obnoxious encounter with her grandmother.

Her thoughts were inward, not at all on her surroundings. So she was surprised to look out the window, what seemed hours later, to find that they were still driving in Edinburgh, with the buildings of the campus within sight.

Anika commented, "I am hungry. How much longer are we going to drive before we leave for my grandmother's?"

Still sensitive to her pain, and wishing to appear heroic, he made a dramatic move.

"I-I-I think I have it now!" he blurted, "This way. It is this way."

He turned sharply left into a narrow alley between two four-story buildings. It was not the pleasantest strip of pavement in the grand old city. It had the smell of a skip bin, what in America they call a dumpster, which had been countless times emptied and never once cleaned. It was narrow and had to be driven slowly. Each column of bricks was dingier than the one before, as they crept their way deeper and darker forward.

Anika had one hundred witty protests knocking on the inside of her lips, begging for release. But for some reason she did not understand, her mouth stayed closed and her thoughts stayed silent. A slight squeal escaped her lips when the left mirror of the car scraped against the crusty bricks. But no adjustment could be made in response. The alley had narrowed and seemed narrower ahead. The tiny car could not progress forward.

Wishing to maintain what weak confidence his passenger had in him, the driver offered nervously, "I-I-I know a-a-another way. Let me just go back."

He put the car in reverse, but when he looked in his mirror, he saw that a skip bin blocked his way.

"Well, that is the strangest thing," the driver thought precisely as Anika spoke the very same words.

The driver did not notice, but Anika could have sworn she saw a cat moving the bin, nudging it slightly with its rear end. She turned her attention to her fellow traveler and stared fixedly at him, waiting for some decision to be made.

Finally, she asked, "Are you going to move it or are you expecting me to?"

The slight-figured man was little more capable of budging the skip bin than his juvenile passenger. But he felt the need to act, so he opened his door, knocking it against the wall of the alley. Any man of normal size would have been utterly trapped. But this man was tiny enough to slink through the cracked door.

"Y-y-you s-s-stay here," he recommended with the authority of a mouse, "I-I will get help."

"And directions!" Anika shouted as he closed the door.

He worked his way behind the car and through the slender space between the skip bin and the alley wall. He was gone and Anika was alone in an alley that, against all reason, turned much darker the moment her timid escort was out of sight. Being alone did not concern her. She was relieved by it, and she savored the next few moments of solitude.

It was *only* a few moments before the pitter-patter of cat paws drummed across the roof of the car. The sunlight should have continued to light the alley from above. Not so many hours had passed in the attempt to leave the city. Whether from the sudden onset of thick clouds or from *any* source natural or unnatural, it appeared as twilight within the alley, and the sky above was so dark that Anika could not see the tops of the four-story buildings that enclosed her, as she twisted and contorted to look upward through the back window.

The cat leaped from the roof to land on the hood of the car. It drew Anika's sharp glance, and they met eyes for a single second before it bounded off of the car and disappeared into the darkness. In that second, its face shone from a light that seemed to come from its collar, as it blinked both eyes at her. The collar was less like a pet's collar than like a fashion accessory, a dark tie from which everything around it was made brighter.

Anika had heard pet owners boast of the abundance of personality to be found in the domestic animal kingdom. She had heard of how dogs, cats, hamsters, even snakes and turtles express themselves. She never paid it much mind. But this cat, this one cat in the darkness looked at her with playful longing, beckoning her to follow. Whether her next steps were motivated by that furry expression, or by the rude little man who had left her there, or by the cramped quarters of the tiny car, it is difficult to say, but Anika squeezed out of the car as the man had done. She did not maneuver her way between the skip bin and wall, but went the *other* way, toward the front of the car, in pursuit of the cat.

Anika pressed on and on, what felt like several city blocks, without seeing an end to the alley. The darkness closed in oppressively and she had no source of light to guide her. She kicked empty boxes and bumped her knees on hard things she could not identify. She heard the sound of a creaking door and spun in all directions to pick up its location. The alley went silent again and Anika had no idea which way she was facing, whether the car sat to her left or right. If not for gravity holding her feet firmly to the ground, she would not have known up from down. She squatted where she stood and began to cry.

"Don't cry, my friend," came a soft, boyish voice to her left.

She turned toward it, and there, an arm's reach from her, was the mysteriously lit face of the cat. It held quite still, and she was able to see it more clearly than before. The collar was no collar at all, but a bow tie of rich and regal blue.

"Were you speaking to me?" Anika tentatively asked the cat.

"Of course I was speaking to you," the cat answered, "Who else is here?"

Anika felt the need to answer the cat's question but was dumbfounded, and only managed to answer, "I-I-I..."

"Come now, dear one," the cat calmed her, "There is no need to fret. You want out of this alley and I can show you the way."

At the offer to escape the alley, Anika shed all befuddlement from being addressed so by a dapper cat, and she responded gleefully, "You can guide me out of the alley? I would appreciate that very much."

"I know this alley well," he bragged, "I could dance it blindfolded."

He bowed low to her, which she returned with a curtsy. He turned away from her, took a few steps forward, looked back to see she was not following, and he shrugged his head in the direction he was walking. She obeyed and traced his steps as nearly as she could, close enough behind him to have reached forward and stroked his tail.

They had not walked far in this way, perhaps a dozen paces, when Anika became sensitive to a dim, yellow light in front of them. As they continued toward it, the alley began to turn brighter, as if the sun had gone bored of its game of hide-and-seek. She could see the cat clearly. He was an orange cat with a round, comfortable face and a neatly tied bowtie. As they continued walking, the alley went bright, quite normal for the time of day. Anika looked up to see that the sky above her was still black, and she still could not see the tops of the four-story buildings. The light did not come from above her. It did not appear to come from in front of her, but seemed rather to come from each breath of air around her.

The cat led Anika to the end of the alley. There was no street waiting for her, no intersection with passing cars and pedestrians. There was only another wall, as dark above as the tops of the walls beside her.

As relieved as she was by the light, Anika was distressed by the dead end, and she frighteningly challenged the cat, "You said you would lead me out of the alley."

"And so I have," answered the cat calmly, "or will have, in a few more steps. Come. We are almost there."

The cat strutted to the far wall of the alley. Against it was the facade of a miniature mansion. It had columns as tall as Anika on either side of a door that was about hip-high on her. It looked out of place embedded into the dingy bricks of an alley wall. Oh but it was gorgeous, and it gleamed in rays of white, silver, and gold. The door was deep brown oak.

"Is that the way?" Anika asked, pointing to the small door, "the way out of the alley."

A raspier voice came from behind her, "It is the way out of everything you wish to escape."

Anika turned quickly and saw another cat, orange like the first, with an identical bowtie, but with a slimmer face and a hint of chaos in the eyes.

The first cat cleared his throat to regain Anika's attention. She turned toward him to see him in a low bow as he introduced himself, "My name is Edward."

"And I am Kenneth," said the cat behind her.

"It does not matter what your name is, not to this one," Edward scolded, "It is my turn. This one is mine."

"Oh settle yourself, Edward," Kenneth spoke indignantly, "There is no harm in us tagging along."

"Us?" Anika questioned, turning back and forth between the two cats.

Edward stood on his hind legs and gestured to Anika's right, "Kenneth is my brother, and those are my sisters."

From out of nowhere, three more orange cats appeared. They wore white bonnets with lace trim of the same rich blue. They danced and spun on their hind legs, in perfect unison with each other, while humming a tune that was in perfect gorgeous harmony. It was a sweet sound, and the dancing was so elegant and complemented the voices perfectly. Anika was spellbound. Kenneth took one strong step toward Anika, stood upon his back legs, adjusted his tie, and bowed to her. She curtsied in return, but not slowly and reverently, as she had to Edward. There was something in Kenneth's eyes and in his voice that forbade her to peel her eyes downward.

Edward cleared his throat again, "Achhh-ah-ah-hem! What do you think you are doing?"

Believing Edward to be addressing her, Anika began a defensive answer, "I am doing just what you told—"

She was interrupted by Kenneth's answer to the question that was addressed to him, "Doing, brother? I am simply bowing to your... to your..."

"To my new friend," Edward finished quickly.

"So this is your *friend*," Kenneth teased, "Alright then, what is your friend's name?"

The question was meant to put Edward on the spot, but it served more to embarrass Anika, who realized at that moment that she had not properly introduced herself to her rescuer.

She turned sheepishly away from Kenneth and toward Edward, and said, "Thank you Edward for helping me. My name is Anika."

Kenneth scoffed jeeringly, "Some friend."

Edward reminded him, "It is my turn. This one is mine."

Kenneth argued, "The last one did not work out. It should still be my turn."

Both cats hissed at each other, while the three sisters continued to dance to their own song.

Anika much preferred Edward to Kenneth, but she did not care much which of them led her from the alley, and she interrupted them, "Gentlemen, I'm sure you both know the alley well and can guide me back to the streets. All other things being equal, I would prefer that Edward finish what he has begun."

"That is fine, then," Kenneth grunted, "but I claim what he cannot finish. I am not sure he still has the stomach for it."

Anika thought that strangely expressed, but she was ready to accept Kenneth's help if Edward's guidance should fail.

"That is a deal, Mr. Kenneth," Anika returned, trying to please both brothers, "But I am sure Edward will come through for me."

"For *you?*" Kenneth remarked with a roll of his eyes, "Yes, I suspect he might come through for *you.*"

Kenneth's sarcastic, teasing tone was incongruent with his words, and Anika could make little sense of the bizarre tension between the brothers.

Kenneth looked to Edward. Edward nodded genially to his brother.

"It seems that is settled," Anika announced cheerfully, "May we press onward? People are awaiting me."

Kenneth bowed again and kept his low bow as he walked backward, away from the little door. The sisters danced into oblivion. Their voices lingered in the air after there was no sight of them. Edward returned to all four feet and walked much like a common cat, but with an air of victory in his stride. Anika followed him toward the mansion facade and the little brown door at its center.

Part Two:

The Rubbish Manor

Edward led Anika closer to the mansion facade. When she was near enough to inspect it closely, she realized that it was made of rubbish, of the sort of things she expected to be found swimming in the smelly sludge at the bottom of an alley skip bin. The columns were made of fish bones and old cans. Worn, discarded shoes, shards of broken dishes, exhausted three-ring binders, wadded up plastic bags, bits of this and that, all old, broken, and discarded, all packed tightly together to make up the outer walls. Despite the revelation of the rubbish, it was still a magnificent sight. It looked rich and quite suitable for an oversized dollhouse in the nursery of any well-to-do family.

Edward swung the door open, bowed low, and gestured inside. Anika smiled, plopped to her hands and knees, and walked like a cat through the door. She had no idea what to expect on the other side, but it certainly was not what greeted her. She found herself in a large room, grander in size and gilded brightness than any room she had ever seen. She stood easily, looked up, and could see no limits to the rising walls. They reached up to a bright and cheery void.

She could determine no source of the bright light that saturated the room — no lamps, no bulbs, no switches, no candles. There were no windows. It shouldn't have mattered if there were windows. The alley beyond the rubbish walls was so dark, a window could have only decreased the brightness. Anika spent only the briefest moment pondering the matter. The delights before her were all-consuming. The light set Edward's orange fur ablaze. In the alley, he appeared much like any cat, except, of course, for his fine conversational skills, his gallant gentility, his ability to move gracefully on his hind legs, and his dapper tie. In the Rubbish Manor, those extraordinary traits were compounded, for he glowed with stately elegance.

Now, Anika loved her life at the university with her father. But it was not an environment designed for childish pleasures. The halls of the university were lovely in their antiquated and opulent architecture, but they did not shout with a youthful voice, "Come play with me!" It was where young people behaved like old people, and where old people pressed their serious, sober thoughts onto the next generation. This room in the Rubbish Manor was also old. Everything in sight was made of old things, discarded by old people. But like Peter Pan, it refused to grow up. It had all been given new life and new purpose, and it all seemed very glad to be there.

There was a long, twisty slide and a tilting board, a swing set, and toppled boxes with dolls and balls and all sorts of toys spilling from them.

"Let us press on," Edward suggested, "There is nothing here that would interest you."

"Are you joking with me?" Anika giggled, "This place is wonderful."

"But there are people waiting for you," Edward reminded her.

"My odious little driver probably got lost asking for directions," she snorted through a chuckle, "If it is alright with you, I would like to play here for a while."

Edward stood on his hind legs, tilted his head to one side and asked, "Are you quite certain? I think we should move you forward."

Anika knelt in front of him, looked him in the eyes with a smile, and answered, "I am certain I would like to play with *you*, if you will play with me."

"You want to *play* with me?"

"Of course," she answered with a friendly scratch behind his ear, "Isn't that why we are here, to play in this wonderful place?"

Edward seemed at a loss, and he stumbled through his thoughts, "I.. I... I don't play. I mean to say that I haven't played..."

"Edward!" she spoke in a surprised half-sigh, "This is your house. Look around you."

He obeyed her and scanned his face in a full circle. His eyes glowed with wonder, as if he was seeing the magnificence of the Rubbish Manor for the very first time. His eyes rolled gleefully around every twirl in the twisty slide, and leaped over the obstacle course, and swayed in imagination with the swing set.

Anika interrupted, snapping him back to the question at hand, "Edward, will you play with me?"

Edward dropped to his front paws, let out an excited meow, and sprinted to the tilting board. He pulled his side to the floor and mounted. Anika's squeal sounded much like Edward's meow. She followed and pushed her side of the board down, lifting Edward into the air. She sat and shoved the floor with her legs, sending her upward and Edward downward. Edward was perched on his side, unable to push against the floor. He did not need to. Anika's weight brought her back down with a thud, popping Edward off of the board to float for an instant above his seat. He landed with a laugh, and Anika pushed herself up again.

Each time Edward flew into the air and landed back on his seat, he squinted his eyes and let out a chirping purr. And with each chirping purr, Anika laughed and snorted uncontrollably.

She recovered just enough to shout, "Oh my goodness, I have never played on one of these before. This is so much fun!"

Each thrust of her legs was too exciting and too hilarious to be the last, and on and on they went. Twenty minutes, forty, maybe a full hour, Anika could not have said how long they went up and down on the tilting board. When at last she had had enough, she stepped off of her end. In the absence of an opposing weight, Edward's end fell hard to the floor. Before it hit, he leaped from it to Anika. She caught him in her arms, high upon her chest. His whiskers tickled her cheek.

Anika was tremendously grateful to him. Not only did he rescue her from the dark alley. He brought her to the wonderful Rubbish Manor and played with her like no *human* ever had. With no forethought, responding to her swell of emotion, she squeezed him tightly and kissed him on his head. Edward's purr in response was so forceful that it reverberated through Anika's rib cage.

He suddenly shook, as if a terrible memory kicked down the door of his mind and announced itself threateningly. It startled Anika, and she dropped him to the floor.

"What is it?" Anika asked in a panic, "Should I not have kissed you. I am sorry. I didn't mean to."

Edward's wide eyes shortened and his pleasant, round face relaxed. "Oh no, no, no," he answered, "I rather enjoyed it."

"What is it?" she asked, "You frightened me."

"It is nothing, only that I was having such a good time with you that I almost forgot... That is, I suddenly remembered that you... what I..."

The singing voices of the sisters rose from some unknown direction. The sound was less pleasant to Anika's ears than before. It was somehow shriller, not quite irritating, but not dulcet.

Kenneth's voice came loudly and clearly from Anika's right to finish Edward's thought, "Where you are supposed to be leading her... kind brother? Perhaps you have forgotten the way. Maybe you should return to the alley and let me take her from here."

Edward's kind face turned sour. He squinted, raising his nose to his eyes, growled, and reminded Kenneth, "Absolutely not. You know well that it is my—"

"Yes, yes," Kenneth interrupted, "it is your turn. This one is yours. Get on with it or forfeit your... *friend.*"

"Please don't be cross, Kenneth," Anika begged, "I am in no hurry. I asked Edward if I could stay, and I asked him to play with me."

Kenneth bowed to her and said, "Of course, well, I am his older brother. It is my duty to look after him."

Edward scoffed, "You are older by one minute."

"One and a half," Kenneth corrected.

Edward wanted nothing to do with the petty details of their births, and he snapped, "I know what I am doing. I have done this before."

"Clearly you have," retorted Kenneth, "You are growing plump, much plumper than I."

"Yes, well, there you have it. You are no cat to be telling me how to..."

"How to?" Kenneth prompted, winking at Anika.

"How to guide my friend correctly."

Kenneth softened and yielded, "As long as you take your friend where she should be taken, I leave it to you, *little* brother."

"Where I should be taken?" Anika turned to Edward and asked.

Edward shook, drew a deep breath, sat like a house cat, with his tail wrapped around his front paws, and answered in a calm, low voice, "Where you *wish* to be taken."

Edward and Kenneth nodded cordially to each other, and Kenneth turned and trotted behind a twisty slide. As he crossed behind a post, he did not appear on the other side, like he was sucked into some invisible hole. The voices of the singing sisters faded in all directions. Anika gave the phenomenon little thought. She was uncomfortable with the tension between the brothers, and the sisters had not exactly endeared themselves to her. She was relieved to have Edward again to herself.

Edward, as much his calm and pleasant self as ever, strolled to one of the toppled boxes of spilled toys. He sat beside a ball and invited encouragingly, "If you are truly in no hurry..."

He placed his paw on the ball and rolled it to Anika.

Anika caught it under her foot and said, "I am truly in no hurry, but maybe I should be. I don't know how late it is, or even what day it is. Do you know, Edward, how long we have played together?

Edward answered in verse,

Proud Maisie is in the wood,

Walking so early;

Sweet Robin sits on the bush,

Singing so rarely.

Anika shouted gleefully, "Edward! You know Walter Scott!"

Edward's eyes widened to consume most of his face. His mouth hung open for a full count of five before he closed it and exclaimed, "And so, my friend, do you!"

"Yes, I do," she responded with pride, "I know Walter Scott and many others. My father, you see, he reads..." She turned visibly melancholy, lowered her head, and finished, "My father *used* to read to me, and I to him. But he has died, and I have nobody."

Edward hummed in sympathetic contemplation.

After a short, silent pause, Anika perked up. She turned her eyes fixedly at Edward and remarked, "Well that is not true, is it? You are my friend. That is what you said. You are my friend, Edward. I have you, and I am very happy to have you. I am certainly in no hurry to leave my only friend. It is so much fun here. Let's play."

Edward winced and shriveled his posture to half its normal height, as if stabbed with a sharp pain. Anika rolled the ball forward with her foot. Edward received it and rolled it back. Anika grinned widely and sent it toward her friend with greater force. Before it reached Edward, it was stopped by the stomping paw of Kenneth. Although there were no shadows on the floor, and the light seemed to come from

every direction at once, half of Kenneth
appeared as if shadowed. He looked like
two halves of different cats glued together,
one darker than the other, with sharper,
leaner features and a devilish look about
the eyes and mouth.

"Is it play time again?" he asked in a mockingly light tone, as he took a step backward, away from the ball.

As he backed away, he was fully lit again and looked entirely as he had before. He left the ball where he had stopped it, right between Anika and Edward. The wheezing song of the sisters' singing rose to an almost unbearable level. It was much more grating, and it sounded like twice as many cats. They appeared from behind Anika, dancing, twirling, and leaping. One of them knocked the ball without noticing, and without in any way disturbing their song and dance. The ball flew out of sight. The sisters knocked the toy box and scattered the toys beyond reach. They twirled on, giving no notice to anything or anyone around them, until their twirling bodies and increasingly creaking voices were gone again.

That left Anika and the brothers, and she was not in the mood to witness another bickering squabble, not after having so recently recovered from sadness.

"Enough, you two!" she exclaimed in an uncharacteristically maternal tone, "I have come to understand that it is Edward's turn, and have begun to play at ball with him. I *will* play with him, then I will play with you, Kenneth. Really, I don't mind being shared."

Kenneth grinned devilishly at his brother and said, "What are the rules, Edward, if the... *friend* asks to be shared? I think that you must share her."

"Truly," Anika began to answer, "I don't mind being—"

While still staring Kenneth down with a furiously writhing face, Edward shushed Anika violently, which jolted her heart with surprise. He turned to her, and all harshness melted from his expression.

Kenneth walked closer to his brother and carefully examined his gaze at Anika. He straightened Edward's bow tie, sat back, and said, "Ohhh I understand now. I see clearly why you take so long. You like this one."

"You see nothing!!!" Edward shouted, again shocking Anika with his violence.

Anika had no idea what to make of it all. She couldn't understand Kenneth's hurry to move her along. Perhaps the brothers had plans that her visit to their alley had delayed. She did not like being the source of so much tension between them. But she also was not so very eager to leave Edinburgh and retire to a life of boredom on a farm with her grandmother.

She addressed Kenneth, "I see that you want to move me along. Please tell me why. Have I offended you?"

"Perhaps I should let you delay," Kenneth teased Edward, ignoring Anika's question "Your friend appears to have grown since you found her. Now there is more of her, too much *friend* for you. Play with her some more, and then we can share."

Anika interjected, "There are plenty of things here to play with. The tilting board is a game for two, but there are many things that we can all do together."

"She is right," Kenneth addressed Edward, "There are things we could do together, just the three of us."

"No!" Edward demanded, as the hair rose across his back, "These are not your decisions. It is my turn. This one is mine."

"Fine, brother, fine," Kenneth yielded, "Have it your way. Lead her on or stay and play. It is all the same to me."

Edward nodded, suspicious of Kenneth's sudden deference. Anika had been in their company long enough to know that yielding to Edward was not in Kenneth's nature, and she was equally suspicious. Still, Edward was willing to take the victory however it came. He decided to remain where they were for a while. There were still toys to play with, slides to ride down, and most importantly to Edward, poetry to recite.

For hour upon hour they played. They jumped and slid and bounced balls of many shapes, sizes, and colors. They played language games like *The Minister's Cat*. Anika could not remember having so much fun. Often, during the quieter moments of their play, she caught herself staring at Edward and thinking how very much like her father he is, particularly when he passionately quoted some Scottish writer or another.

At last, Anika was hungry. She had given no thought to food since she mentioned her hunger to the timid little driver. During the final round of *The Minister's Cat*, her stomach growled so loudly that Edward thought it was her voice mumbling her answer.

He began, "The minister's cat is a *gregarious* cat."

She returned, "The minister's cat is a— *Grrrrummmble*."

He tilted his head and perked his ears as he challenged her answer, "I don't know that word. Are you sure it is official?"

She did not answer, but only looked down to her stomach. His eyes followed and the sound came again, "*Grrrrummmble*."

With concerned embarrassment, he said, "Oh my, you are hungry. How unthoughtful of me. I have never had to feed one of... What I mean is, I don't often have dinner guests here."

"Yes," Kenneth's voice came from behind Anika, "It is very unthoughtful, ignoring the hunger of others."

Ever accompanying Kenneth came again the three sisters, dancing and twirling. Anika was struck by their appearance. They were thinner than before, much thinner, and their voices were both shrill and painfully out of tune with one another. They also seemed shorter than before, as did Kenneth.

"I believe Kenneth is right," Anika thought to herself, "I have grown."

She looked down to her trouser cuffs and saw that they rode higher up her legs.

"I have grown!" she exclaimed aloud, "I must have been here a *very* long time."

The thought reminded of her need to eat. She thought it strange that she had not done so earlier. It felt to her like she had been in the Rubbish Manor for many days, perhaps weeks... or longer.

The increasingly gaunt sisters danced toward her with plates in their paws. Things were piled upon the plates, steaming things that put off a succulent aroma. Kenneth gestured to the floor in front of Anika, and she responded by plopping to a seat where she stood. The sisters danced across her, each placing two plates in front of her. The plates had writing scribbled on them in haphazard patterns and angles, and typing with highlighted lines and scratched out lines. Upon closer examination, Anika saw what they really were. They were term papers and reports, personal letters and memos, all discarded by their human owners and repurposed by the alley cats. They were layered and folded into fancy, star-shaped dishes that could have been used without complaint in any literature-themed restaurant of the highest quality.

Anika leaned into the plates to investigate the source of the succulent steam. It was, like everything else in the Rubbish Manor, well... rubbish. It was clearly pieces of discarded portions, half-consumed by God-knows-whom. But the cats arranged it into a fabulous presentation. Nothing had been served to her from the university cafeteria that looked or smelled so enticing, and she was very hungry. She tried not to think of the dirty places from whence it was scavenged.

As she stared at the plates, Kenneth asked her, "Is our food not to your liking? If you only taste it, you will find that it is more enjoyable to the tongue than to the eye."

"Oh, please don't mistake me," she excused herself fraudulently, "I was only thinking of how lucky I am to be served a meal in the home of my new friends. The food is very enjoyable to my eyes and nose.

My jealous tongue is just waiting for its turn."

"Yes, certainly. I understand that," Kenneth spoke as he turned to Edward, "It is difficult to wait for your turn. I think your eyes and nose should be less selfish."

Kenneth's glare was stern, and Edward turned his head to avoid it.

Kenneth looked back to Anika and continued, "Best not to be unfair. Let your tongue share with your other senses."

That was all the invitation Anika needed. She took a piece of food and put it quickly to her mouth. It was delicious, a unique variety of flavors never dared by the most experimental chefs. Somehow, the tastes complimented each other. It was scrumptious. As quickly as the first bite went in, the next dozen followed. Anika devoured the entire meal.

When she finished, she looked up to see Kenneth and the sisters seated in front of her, each leaning forward and licking their lips. They looked thinner and very hungry.

"Oh no!" Anika exclaimed, "I have eaten it all and left none for you."

Kenneth pulled his tongue back into his mouth and assured her, "Don't you worry. What my sisters served to you was for you alone. We will be eating later."

Anika's look of remorse remained on her face as she said, "Are you sure? I feel terrible. I was just so very hungry."

"It was all meant for you... our friend," Kenneth insisted.

He was so calm and confident in his answer that Anika released her concerns. The sisters still sat staring at her, until Kenneth lifted a paw in the air and shooed them away. In a flash, they stood in unison and began dancing and singing as before. They twirled out of sight, singing an increasingly wretched melody.

"Are they okay?" Anika asked Kenneth, "They sounded so beautiful at first."

Kenneth squinted teasingly at her and asked, "Do they not sound beautiful to you now?"

Anika turned bright red with embarrassment and tried to soften her words, "No, no..., I mean yes. It is just that their voices were so soft before and now I wonder if they are unwell. They still sound beautiful."

Kenneth winked at her and said, "No they do not. I am only teasing you."

He looked to Edward, who sat sulkingly, and he addressed him, "Who could sound well when forced to suffer as they do?"

The moment turned somber with that question, and absolute silence followed. Anika's embarrassment blended with an equal portion of compassion, though what exactly the sisters were suffering, she could not guess.

Kenneth, in a suddenly light tone, leaned into her, within a whisker of her nose, as said, "I do hope you enjoyed your meal and are fully satisfied. It seems that you have done all there is to do in this room, perhaps it is time to move onward. Other rooms await and there is much more fun to be had."

A blur of orange fur flashed away from her, and Kenneth was as comprehensively gone as his suffering sisters.

Edward had been awkwardly inward and silent during the entire exchange with Kenneth. But there they were, alone again, Anika and Edward. She stood slowly and asked her playmate, "Are there other rooms, as Kenneth said? Is there more fun for us to have together? I am not ready to leave you and go to my grandmother's farm. Please take me to the next room, Edward. Please play with me."

Edward's sullen spirits rose with a vengeance. He sprang to his feet, ran two quick circles around Anika, and invited, "My brother is correct. There is much more to do in the inner room, games I have not played in a long time. Yes! I agree. We should move onward and play together."

Part Three:

The Inner Room

Edward led Anika on a long walk. Wide columns hung downward from an infinite upwardness, but did not connect to the floor. They stopped well above Anika's head. As the walk went on, all things were left behind, all toys and play equipment, all walls, even the hanging columns. There was only bright emptiness in all directions. Anika could determine no horizon where the bright floor ended and the vast emptiness beyond began.

There was quite literally nothing to look at. But in such goodly company, what need is there of such things? Their conversation rolled through a vast variety of topics, from the minute to the profound. On more than one occasion, during a rare lull in the talking and quoting, Anika thought of the time. How long had it been since she walked through the darkening alley and met Edward? It seemed like hours since they last encountered Kenneth and the sisters. Anika would have sworn that if their current conversation had occurred at a cafe window, they would have witnessed the fall and rise again of the sun at least once.

Finally, he led her to a distant wall, at the bottom of which was another wooden door. This door was much smaller than the one that opened from the alley. Anika could not simply drop to her knees and walk through it like a cat. Edward opened the door and went through first. The hairs of his back brushed against the top of the low doorway.

Anika called to him from her side, "I will never fit through that door. I am too big, especially now that I have grown so much."

She looked down to her trousers and saw the hems higher upon her legs than before.

"No," she proclaimed, "No, I will never fit through such a tiny door."

A high, piercing ring came into her head. She pushed the heels of her palms firmly against her ears, believing her ears to be ringing. The sound stopped, but when she removed her hands, it picked up again, louder than before. Her ears were not ringing. They were perceiving the sound of the sisters' horrid song. Directly behind her, as instantly as he disappeared before, Kenneth sat licking his paw.

He whispered to her, "You want to get to Edward, I imagine."

"I do. Do you know another way?"

"There is no other way, just as there is no way backward. You will have to go through this door."

"You are silly!" she exclaimed.

With those words, the wretched ringing of the sisters' voices stopped. They twirled from out of nowhere to stop in low curtsies to Anika. They froze there like statues, staring at the floor in front of them.

"I am not a silly cat," Kenneth answered, "There is only room here for one of those and Edward seems to have claimed it. No, I am in earnest."

"Edward is kind," Anika came back defensively, "He is smart and well-read, and he is fun to play with."

"Whatever you say, but he has gone through the door and not shown you how to follow him. I bet he is strolling and prattling on with his useless quotations and human philosophy, believing you to be right beside him."

The aspersion did not have its intended effect. The image of Edward conversing with the air, believing his friend to be at his side, only adhered him more tightly to

Anika's affection. She giggled and held her hand to her heart.

Kenneth tried again, "I will be the one to help you through the door. Edward has abandoned you. It is my turn."

"Very well," she consented, "I have wanted to be your friend since I met you. There is room in my heart for you too, Kenneth."

He bowed to her with sharp eyes toward her and a fiendish smile, as he replied, "And there is room in me for you."

"So," she said lightly, "how do I get through this door?"

"It is simple," he answered plainly, "You go through."

"But how? I cannot fit."

"Can you fit one arm through?"

"Well, yes. Of course I can fit one arm."

"What about the other? Do you think you could fit the other?"

"If I can fit the one, I can fit the other. My arms are the same size."

"And what about your foot, your leg? Do you think you could fit a leg through?"

"Yes, I believe so."

"How about the other leg?"

"Yes, yes. But what good would that do me?"

"How about your head? I think if you lay low, you could squeeze your head through."

"Yes, I am certain I could. But—"

Kenneth interrupted and proposed, "If each of your parts will fit, simply put them through one at a time."

Anika cocked her head to one side, lowered her eyebrows sternly, crossed her arms at her chest and said, "That is ridiculous."

"Is it?" Kenneth asked.

The three sisters rose from their curtsies. They each looked at Anika and spoke to her for the very first time, asking in unison, "Is it?"

Anika relaxed her disapproving pose and begged, "Please, Kenneth, do not tease me. Edward will be wondering where I am. How worried will he be when he sees I am not beside him?"

Kenneth sat high and proud. The sisters assumed the exact same posture in a row behind him.

One sister spoke, "Edward will be worried."

Another followed, "Yes, very worried."

The third offered in quick succession, "How very worried he will be."

Anika began to fret dearly, and she suggested, "You can fit through the door easily, Kenneth. Will you go through and tell him that I am stuck on this side?"

"Tisk, tisk, tisk," he said with a shake of his head, "He does not want to see me. It had better come from you."

Anika gestured to the tiny door and then to herself, head to toes.

Kenneth suggested, "Only put your head through and shout for him. Perhaps you will be able to see where he is."

It was not a bad idea. Anika thanked Kenneth, sprawled flat on her belly, and put her head through the door. She could not turn her head, so she could not see much but the floor. There were indistinct structures in her peripheral vision, but no movement and no rambling quotations.

She began to shout, "Edwa—" but stopped sharp when she saw her own right hand slide by her face. She could feel the multiple paws behind her pushing it through. Once her right arm was extended beside her face, her left followed behind. She saw a familiar shoe, her shoe, still embracing her right foot as her leg shot up beside her. It seemed to be boneless and crawling through on its own.

"You see!" came Kenneth's voice, muffled from behind her, "One part at a time."

Her left leg followed the right. Such an impossibly contorted position she must have been in, with her arms and legs pushed through the door beside her head. There was a pop sound, like the uncorking of a bottle, and Anika found herself lying on her belly, shaped quite normally, entirely on Edward's side.

She rose to her feet, squatted as low as she could and looked through the door. There sat Kenneth.

"You see?" Kenneth said proudly, "I am not such a bad guide, am I? When you find Edward, tell him that it was I who got you through."

Anika could not see deeply through the door. She could not see the sisters. But she heard them say together, "Kenneth got her through the door. Kenneth got her through the door."

Those words repeated and turned from spoken to sung. Perhaps "sung" is a poor choice of words. They were by no definition melodic. Their words transformed to their usual singing, higher, shriller, and more grossly out of tune than ever. They must have danced away, for their noise faded, leaving only Kenneth on the other side.

"Thank you Kenneth," Anika said sincerely, "Won't you come with me, at least until I find your brother?"

"Oh no. I do not think that would be best. But do tell him that *I* got you through, and that he should listen more closely to me."

"I *will* tell him," she promised, "And thank you, Kenneth. Thank you very much."

He gave no response. He simply closed the door between them, leaving Anika to explore the inner room and search for Edward.

The search required some effort. The inner room was no vacant expanse. It was cluttered with many exciting things to do, with many things among which a cat and a girl can be separated and lost from one another. The most obvious feature was a hill in the center of the room, a gently sloped mound from the top of which swirled downward a toboggan run. Empty one-person, wheeled toboggan sleds rolled down the track in steady progression. From where she stood just inside the door, Anika could not see the beginning of the track nor the end, so she could not tell where the sleds came from, where they went, or who, if anybody, was setting them and sending them.

A walking path wound around the slope, bridging over the track in places and tunneling under it. The beginning of the path was marked by a grand arch at the base of the slope. In the absence of any other ideas, this seemed to Anika to be her best way forward. She passed under the arch and onto the path, playing referee between her own organs, which could not agree on what to focus upon. Finding Edward was the goal of her brain. Her eyes were more interested in the delights around her, and her heart was torn between the two.

Along the path, there were hardly five short paces between attractions. Unmanned snack booths offered bite-sized portions of discarded confections, all appearing as splendid as if they still sat in the confectioner's window. Petit fours sat in military formations, displaying every gradient of a pastel rainbow. These were *not* half-eaten refuse scrounged from the floor of an alley. They were pristine — mere hours beyond their expiration for sale. Each booth was followed closely by another, each boasting proudly of its theme, from snacks to carnival games, each eerily empty and silent. The only sound in the room was the incessant rolling of the sleds down the track.

As with everything else in the Rubbish Manor, each thing that paraded before Anika's eyes, or shouted at her ears, or brazenly stormed its way into her nose had been discarded by the humans of Edinburgh, salvaged by God-knows-whom, brought to the narrow alley, and placed masterfully within the manor. Anika looked back at the tiny door, still barely within her sight, and she wondered at how so many things very large and small could have come through. Surely the track and the sleds, the booths and the arch, could not have been folded and crammed through by Kenneth and his sisters, the way she had been. That fleeting thought of Kenneth and his sisters brought Anika's mind back to Edward, who had very firmly become her dearest friend.

The sudden recollection of her friend sent from her mouth, in an abrupt and panicked outburst, "Edward, where are you?"

In a soft, calm, and pleasing voice from directly behind her came his reply, "Never too far from you, dear friend."

"I should hope not," she said through her brightening face, "Without you, I would be lost. Afterall, it *is* your turn. I am yours."

He sighed, and every muscle in his body went weak with emotion, as he said, "That you are, very dear one. That you are."

Anika and Edward went directly for the top of the toboggan run, bypassing many games and booths without a glance. The sleds fit Anika perfectly, with precisely enough room for one dapper cat on her lap. There may have been twenty, perhaps thirty different sleds, rolling in constant parade down the winding track, each pieced together from this and that, and painted with different colors and designs. They rode each of them in their turns, then rode them each again before moving on to the room's other attractions. While they flew down the hill, they did not converse. There were no quotations dancing a lively jig from mouth to ear. There was only laughter, hearty laughter, until their bellies ached. It was a very childlike fun, not like anything at the university.

When their heads could not take another run of the toboggan course, they left it behind. They went to a snack booth and helped themselves to the treats on display. The longer Edward was apart from Kenneth, the less cat-like he was. He took fiendish delight in the petit fours, not hunching and devouring them like a house cat at his food bowl, or plundering them like an alley cat at a rubbish can, but lounged against the base of the booth, with one hind leg crossed over the other, and his pinky claw lifted off of the pastry as he delicately nibbled. With each bite, he had a rumbling purr and some paraphrased complement to his meal, extracted from the life work of one dead Scottish author or another. Anika kept pace, matching him treat for treat and quotation for quotation.

For uncounted and unmeasured hours they went on, alternating between game booths and food booths, eating so they could play and playing to build the appetite to eat some more. Edward was anything but gaunt, like his siblings. He was stuffed with treats and increasingly fluffy. Anika wanted to ask him why his brother and sisters were so underfed when such delicious foods were so readily available. She dared not do so and pull her dear friend from his very happy, very human, very boy-like mood. On many occasions during their vast time in the inner room,

Anika thought of her father. She could not have helped it. Edward was much like him. He recited his quotations with silly contortions of the face and in a variety of vocal tones, much as her father used to read to her. In Edward's company, she kept her connection to Fergus, and the sting of her loss was lessened.

Anika and Edward came to a game booth that had stacked brass canisters with balls to throw and knock them over. Edward was exceedingly good at this game, and he had to back himself farther and farther from his targets with each turn, just to challenge himself. Anika stood in the booth and restacked the canisters each time Edward threw the ball. He backed so far from the booth that Anika, squinting and straining to focus, could not have known him from a badger. He threw the ball from that great distance and missed the booth entirely. The ball flew over Anika, over the booth, and rolled down the slope on the other side.

"I will get it!" Anika shouted to Edward.

She ran behind the booth and followed the path of the ball. She crossed over the walking path and jumped over the toboggan track where it intersected her. She ducked around other booths, all at top speed in pursuit of the ball. At the bottom of the hill, she came to a wall. The ball was not there. She looked to her left and right but could not see it. With no guidance but a blind hunch, she turned to the right and followed the wall.

She came to a tiny door. Forgetting the ball, she stopped and stared at it. It was identical to the wooden doors she had already seen in the Rubbish Manor, but much, much smaller. It was hardly taller than one of her feet placed heel to the floor and toes pointed upward. Each door opened to her, since she met the cats in the alley, offered more magnificent delights, so it is no wonder that the tiny door intrigued her.

She squatted down to get a closer look at it, when the missing ball rolled along the wall from her right and stopped in front of the door.

"I believe you were looking for this," came Kenneth's voice from the same direction.

Anika smiled at him. Whether or not he meant to play, he rolled a ball to her, and she took it as an invitation.

"Thank you, Kenneth," she spoke tentatively. She picked up the ball, dropped to a seat facing him, and rolled the ball back to him.

Kenneth let it roll right past him, as if he was blind to it.

He asked, "Don't you want to know what is on the other side of that door?"

"It is another room, I presume."

"Would you like to see for yourself?"

"Kenneth, this door is much smaller. I could never go through it like I went through the last one, even with your help. I don't think I could fit any of my parts through that door."

"Nevertheless," he responded, "it is the way you must go, the only way, if you ever wish to leave this room."

She stood straight and even taller than before, looking down at the door as she commented, "I do not want to stay here forever, but I might have no choice, if this is truly the only way out. I will never fit through that door."

"There is a way to get you through, only one way, and if you ever want to leave this room, that is how it must be done."

"No, no, no, no!" came Edward's frantic voice from behind Anika, "Not yet. No, no, not yet!"

Kenneth sat comfortably and scratched behind his ear. He drew a long inhale and let the breath out with the question, "If not now, brother, when? You know it has to happen. It might as well happen now."

It was an ominous choice of words, and Anika was not at all comfortable. Looking back and forth between the brothers, she asked, "What has to happen."

"It's very simple," Kenneth responded, "You have to go through that door, and as I told you, there is only one way for that to happen. Isn't that right, Edward?"

Anika looked down to Edward, whose eyes widened and watered. His lower jaw quivered, and he affirmed, "There is only one way for you to get through that door... But not yet, not now, not now. I cannot..."

Edward mumbled unintelligibly, as if in great shock from some horrible event. He shook himself out of his stupor and snapped at Kenneth, "Why are you here? It is my turn. Anika is mine. Get out of here! Leave us alone! Go back to the alley! You don't belong here!"

Kenneth shook his head calmly, in stark contrast to the panic that had overtaken Edward, and he spoke in a low and slow voice, "The Rubbish Manor is as much mine as yours. Find me the rule that says I cannot be here. I have the right to be here, and I have the right to advise our friend. I am doing what we have always done. What are you doing?"

Edward drew several deep breaths, slowing and calming with each exhale. He rubbed his eyes with both paws, sat proudly, released a long sigh, and spoke, "Carmichael writes of the ability to pursue one's own interests without infringing on the rights of another. You ask what I am doing. I am doing just that. You know it is my turn. Anika is mine. What difference should it make to you how long I should spend with her and how we should pass that time? She is, as Carmichael would say, my interests, not yours. Your rights are not infringed upon by me."

Kenneth arched his back and hissed, then melted back into a calmer posture, before saying harshly, "You know I do not give a whisker for your Carmichael or any of the dead scribblers you love to quote. This alley does not belong to them. It belongs to us and their words carry no weight here. If you spent more time here with us and much less under the tables of the coffee houses, being hand-fed your treats, you would still be with us. Think brother, have you ever brought treats back for me or our sisters?"

"Kenneth," Edward spoke compassionately, "It is not about the treats. I go there for the conversations, if only to overhear them. If you wish me to stay in the alley, you should be glad to keep Anika as long as possible. While she is here—"

He turned to Anika and gave her a smile and wink, then finished, "I am getting all the finest conversation I have ever had. I have no need to go to the coffee houses or anywhere else while she is here."

Kenneth blurted angrily, "But that is not why she was brought to the Rubbish Manor, is it?"

Edward lowered his head and mumbled, "The best laid schemes of mice and men go often askew."

Anika, perceiving Edward's sorrow, asked him, "Since the topic has come up, why have you brought me here? It was not simply to guide me out of the alley and to the street beyond."

"Perceived that, did you?" Kenneth answered for him, "You are right. He took you into the manor to lead you where you *should* be led."

He took an offensive stance and looked like he was ready to pounce on Edward, as he growled, "But he has been disloyal to his family."

The brothers had argued before. Anika was used to that. But their exchanges, as contentious as they had been, were mostly civil. This new tone between them startled and frightened Anika. They both seemed one harsh syllable away from violence, and she stood precariously between them.

Edward became remorsefully sullen in his posture, but demanded in his defense, "I am not disloyal. I am simply exercising my right."

Kenneth snapped, "What right?"

Edward followed with another quotation, "The right which belongs to individuals in the state of nature to claim what is their own."

Anika stomped her foot between them and finished the quotation that she knew very well, "and is conferred upon them for the sake of **civil peace**!"

Kenneth had not played with Anika. He had not conversed with her as Edward had. He had no occasion to exchange passages from Scottish authors. Had he the occasion, he would have been unable to do so. Nevertheless, at her quotation, it was his turn to stagger in disbelief.

"You know Carmichael?" he exclaimed.

Anika winked at Edward while answering Kenneth, "And so now, my friend, do you."

"You see," Edward followed, turning to his brother, "There is more to her than you thought. She is more than either of us hoped she would be. We must treat her differently."

Kenneth sat back, lifted his right hind leg above his head, licked his belly a few times, sat straight again, and came back, "Interesting that you should choose that word... Treat."

"You are pathetic," Edward growled, "and you are blind if you do not see what I see."

Kenneth stood sharply and took a few bold steps toward Edward. When Edward hissed at him defensively, he stopped and said, "I see perfectly, and I smell. But I do not taste."

Anika could make no sense of the hostility. All she knew was that she was at the heart of it, and it embarrassed her and made her nervous. For the first time, she felt a sense of peril, like the Rubbish Manor was not a safe place to be. She folded her arms in front of her and lowered her head, as if trying to hide behind herself. She shivered uncontrollably. It caught Edward's attention.

He walked tightly around her, rubbing his face against her legs and purring. He stopped, facing as she faced, toward Kenneth, and he said in a lofty academic voice, "How can you not see that she is unlike the others. As Hume put it, no one ever threw away life while it was worth keeping. Anika is worth keeping."

Anika, still slouching with folded arms and lowered head, added, "Hume also wrote that beauty in things exists in the mind which contemplates them. I think Kenneth doesn't *contemplate* me as you do."

Kenneth sat passing his gaze between Anika and Edward. He shook his head with a slight giggle, then strolled around Edward saying, "So, it all makes sense to me now. She has grabbed your heart in the one way you are most vulnerable. That would have been perfect if you had met her in one of those coffee houses you cannot keep away from. But she came to the alley and into the Rubbish Manor. There are rules here and you must follow them. She cannot go backward. She must go forward, and there is only one way for her to do that."

"I know that she cannot go backward," Edward argued, "but who said that she must go forward? I never agreed to such a rule. I can think of no reason she cannot stay right here in this room forever, right beside me! It is your turn next. You should forget this one."

Edward rubbed his face on Anika's leg and stood high and proud beside her.

Anika looked down to Edward and disagreed, "I can think of reasons. I see no bed here, and I will someday need to sleep. After all of this time, people must be worried about me. I cannot let them believe that I have disappeared. Edward, you are my best friend. But can't I leave you and come back? Can I at least let my grandmother know that I am alive? Can't I go to the coffee houses with you and meet the people? I am certain I would not like to stay in this room *forever*."

"Well there you have it, Edward," Kenneth blustered, "She does not wish to stay here forever, and there is only one way for her to go forward."

"Now, now, Kenneth," Anika interrupted, "I never said I wished to leave immediately. I have not tired of this room just yet. Edward and I have not fully explored it. I have never been to any place like this in my life and I am not yet eager to leave."

"Then by all means," he replied, "treat yourself. When it is time to cross the next threshold, I will be there to help you as I did before, and then, maybe I will treat *myself*." Then he began to walk away.

Edward snorted. It sounded to Anika like a laugh, but when she looked at him, he was crying. Through his tears he rose tall. He meant business. He must have, for he quoted the great Robert Burns. He fixed his eyes aggressively to his brother, and he recited,

Ha! Where are you going, you crawling

wonder?

Your impudence protects you sorely,

I can not say but you swagger rarely

Over gauze and lace

Kenneth huffed tauntingly, and asked, "Why do you recite it wrongly? Those are not the words."

"Being a sensible cat," Edward returned, "being a gentile cat, one with manners, I speak so that all around me can understand."

"Well," Kenneth came back sneeringly, "if she is everything you say she is, if she is so extraordinary as to break from our traditions, she should need no translation."

Anika giggled and shook her head. She bent low, patted Kenneth on the head like a household pet, and said, "I need no translation. I think your brother was referring to you, not me."

Kenneth scoffed and rolled his eyes, then Anika silenced and stilled him by continuing the Burns stanza in dialect,

Tho' faith! I fear ye dine but sparely

On sic a place

Kenneth patted his paw on the floor in front of him. It was his attempt at sarcastic applause. He followed it by saying, "Well done indeed. She *is* special, Edward. She understands what you do not. As she just admitted, she fears I dine but sparingly."

He had a point. As uncomfortable as he made her, Anika was concerned for Kenneth. He *did* appear to have lost weight.

"Why would you dine sparingly with so much to eat in this place?" she asked him earnestly. "Maybe you should ask your sisters to serve you food as they served me."

Kenneth's smile spread wide and diabolical, as he responded, "Yes, wise girl, I think you are right. I should ask my sisters to serve me my food."

With that, he darted away, out of sight and sound, but not out of mind. A distinct bitterness hung in the air where such a contentious encounter occurred.

Edward tried to shake them both free of it, offering, "Come my dear friend, while our time is ours alone. Let us be as we have been."

Anika needed little coaxing. She ran several steps from Edward, toward the peak of the hill, turned back to him, and gestured him forward with a roll of her head. He sauntered gloomily at first, but her smile quickly intoxicated him. By the time he reached her, he was as giddy as ever, and as eager to play, talk, debate, and quote.

Part Four:

To a Mouse

There was no natural way of telling how long Anika and Edward remained in the inner room together. They visited every booth, many times, and rode the toboggan until the thrill had gone stale. Eventually, even the petit fours were less delightful.

Anika sat on the path, and Edward crawled upon her lap. At last, Anika admitted, "I think I would like to move on now. This has all been wonderful, but I am growing up, and I must have a life outside of the Rubbish Manor."

Edward started to cry, and between gasps, he told her, "My dear Anika, I cannot lose you. I have never had a friend like you, and I am not likely to ever find another."

She ran her hand tenderly across his head and asked him, "Why must you lose me? I will always be your friend, and I'm certain I could find my way back to your alley. But I must move on."

Edward's sobs intensified. Her pity for his sorrow was profound, and she assured him, "Dear Edward, the day before I came to your alley, I lost my dear father. He was all that I loved in this world. When he died, I had nothing. But I met you, and you are very much like him. With you, I feel that I still have a father, and the friend my father always was to me. You will not lose me. You will *never* lose me."

Edward was honored, and he asked her to tell him about her father. He sat enamored on her lap as she recalled all that she could about her father and their time together. In listening, he realized that she was right, that she could not remain in the inner room of the Rubbish Manor forever. She had a life worth resuming and people who loved her. In recounting her life, she began to come to the same conclusion.

Anika told him about the plan to take her to her grandmother's farm, and how desperately she had resented it.

"I too once thought I could never live on a farm," he said to her, "away from the coffee houses and tables, and the fine conversations of the students. I think differently since meeting you, on this and many subjects. A quiet farm with a good friend could provide me all that I desire about the city, and remove from me much of what I despise."

His words struck her silent, in deep thought. After a long pause, he continued, quoting Allan Ramsay,

Gi'e me a lass with a lump of land,

And in my bosom I'll hug my treasure

He lowered his eyes, but looked upward through his brow whiskers to see if she would come back with a quote of her own. She knew Allan Ramsay. Of course she did, and she continued from the same poem, after a thoughtful, vocalized sigh,

Love tips his arrows with woods and

parks,

And castles, and riggs, and moors,

and meadows

They pondered the quotation in unified silence and adoring gazes at each other, then she broke it, saying, "I could take you with me to my grandmother's farm, if you would like to come with me."

He did not answer. He only stared up at her with adoring eyes. Finally, after a curt inhale and a forced exhale, she said, I am ready, Edward. What is this one way forward? How do I get through the tiny door?"

"We have a powder that you must inhale."

"A powder? What does it do? Will it shrink me so I can fit through the door."

"Yes, you will shrink. But there is more. You will be transformed into a mouse."

Anika lifted him from her lap, set him beside her, and scooted away from him. "Oh," she said with a pounding heart, "I see. That is why Kenneth wanted me through. He meant to eat me."

"Yes he did, but he cannot."

"Why can he not?"

"Because my friend, it is my turn. You are mine."

She looked at him with a stone face and asked him in a faltering voice, "Is that why you brought me here, to turn me into a mouse and eat me?"

Edward began to weep again. He confessed through his tears, "Yes. That is why I led you here. But I have long abandoned that scheme. I love you Anika. That is why I have kept you in the rooms."

"And I cannot go backward?"

He shook his head.

"I have no choice but to use the powder and turn into a mouse... in a house full of cats?"

He nodded.

"Edward!! You have doomed me!"

They cried together, neither daring to touch the other.

When there were no more tears to shed, she asked him, "What is beyond the small door? Is there any way for me to leave the Rubbish Manor?"

"Yes," he answered, "There is a door beyond. It leads back to the alley."

"And will I be a mouse forever?"

"No... I don't know... I mean... I imagine it will wear off. None have ever lasted that long."

Chills ran through her as she imagined the other poor victims of the alley cats, but she gathered herself enough to confirm, "But it might wear off, and I will be human again?"

"I believe so."

Anika perked up. She stood quickly and demanded, "Let us go now! while your brother and sisters are away! You can guide me through the other door, into the alley, and I will hide there until I am human again!"

Edward closed his eyes and pondered the plan. He shivered with fear, but saw no other choice. They walked together to the tiny door, and there, set ceremoniously beside it, was a cup of the magical powder. It must have been placed there by Kenneth. Edward looked quickly and alertly in all directions, but saw no sign of his brother or sisters.

"Now! Quickly!" he ordered, "We must do it now!"

"I am ready," Anika answered.

Edward dipped his paw in the cup. When he pulled it out, it glowed sparkling purple. He raised his paw above his head.

Anika stopped him, saying "Wait!"

He looked again in all directions. When he saw no signs of his siblings, he asked her, "What? What is the matter?"

"I just wanted to tell you, before... just in case... well, you know. I just wanted to tell you that I love you and I do not blame you for whatever happens next, even if you should lose yourself and eat me."

Edward squeezed his eyes tightly shut, pinched cruelly in the heart by love and guilt. He opened his eyes again, took one last, long look at her human face, and blew the powder from his paw. She inhaled it, and in an instant, she stood on four little mouse claws, amid a pile of her clothes. Through her mouse eyes, Edward appeared as big as the four-story buildings that framed the alley. He pushed the door open for her, and Anika scurried through.

He followed her through, and as soon as the door closed behind them, the wretched wailing of the three sisters came loudly to their keen ears. It seemed to come from all directions at once. The kindest critic could not call it a song. It was nothing more than the rabid howl of starving cats. Both Anika and Edward ran in circles around themselves, looking in all directions, trying to locate the source of the sound. They froze at the same time, facing the same direction, facing Kenneth.

"Finally," Kenneth said with a sigh, "I thought this day would never come."

The sisters danced out of nowhere to stand behind Kenneth. Kenneth looked thin, but the sisters looked so much worse. Their orange fur looked like paint, brushed directly onto their skeletons. The only part of them that bore signs of life was their eyes, their hungry, staring eyes. They did little more than twitch toward Anika before she turned away and ran for her life.

As she ran, she looked back to see all five cats chasing her, with Edward leading the way.

"I should have known," she panted out loud, "My father is gone and nobody loves me."

Sharp claws landed on the floor in front of her, stopping her abruptly. They were Edward's, and he stood over her. He trapped her on both sides with his paws and lowered his mouth to her. But no hungry fangs showed. He puckered as well as a cat can pucker. He attempted to kiss her on the head, which, in the absence of a proper pair of human lips, he failed. He contented himself with a rub of her mousy whiskers with his own. But she trembled in terror. The screech of the sisters was faint, but growing louder.

"Please, please, Edward," she begged with a whimpering cry, "Don't eat me."

"Eat you?" he returned, "and forgo our intimacy, which I have grown to cherish. I would sooner eat my own eyes with a fork made of my plucked whiskers. You, Anika, are my friend."

Despite the pledge, she was a tiny mouse and he a large cat with sharp claws. She still shook with fear.

He laid himself flat and set his chin on the floor, so that he looked her level in the eye, softened his voice, and said, "Faith is a difficult gift to give, even to a very dear one, when one is in fear for one's life. Please look in my eyes and reach through that. I ask you to believe in the most devoted feelings of an affectionate friend."

She did as he asked. She looked in his eyes and believed him, but still cowered in fear.

"That is very nice to hear," she replied, not fully relieved, "I may be a cherished friend to you, but I am a desired meal to your brother and sisters."

"Never mind them. As I have told my brother many times, it is my turn. You are mine and I may do as I wish with you. What I wish is to be your friend, now and forever."

With that assurance, Anika felt much less vulnerable in her tiny mouse-ish form. But the others closed in on them and were stalking forward behind Edward. There was something chaotic in the wild, thoughtless eyes of the sisters, that defied reason and rejected order.

Anika added, "My friend, I think it will take some excellent persuasion to calm the hunger of your siblings."

She was right, and Edward knew it. A ravenous ray of greed overtook the frolicky faces of the sisters. Their light dancing turned to low stalking, just as their melodic meows had turned discordant and beastly. Kenneth seemed more himself than did his sisters, more his conniving, swindling, treacherously underhanded self.

"My sisters are lost to the frenzy, I'm afraid," Edward confessed as he turned to face the other cats, "I must appeal to Kenneth. He knows the rules, and he will expect me to follow them when it is his—"

He stopped short, hearing Anika's gasp as she imagined the next poor girl or boy to wander into their alley in search of fun things to do.

"Don't you worry," Edward insisted, suddenly turning to her, "If they wish to place a claw on you, they will need to destroy me first, and I do not think it will come to that."

He turned to face his siblings, lowered his shoulders, raised his tail high, and hissed.

Kenneth rose from his stalking stance, brushed his sisters back with a wave of his paw, and spoke calmly, "It is already done, my brother, and since it would be painful for you to eat your friend, leave her to us. Let me do this favor for you, and then it will be your turn again."

It was four cats against one, against one and a small mouse. Edward resorted to the one thing he had in greatest abundance. He turned to Robert Burns,

How dare you set your foot upon her -
Such fine a lady!
Go somewhere else and seek your dinner
On some poor body

He rose taller, and continued louder and sterner,

Brother, attend! whether thy soul
Soars fancy's flights beyond the pole,
Or darkling grubs this earthly hole
In low pursuit;

Know, prudent, cautious, self-control

Is wisdom's root!

A silent pause followed. Anika prayed that the piercing wisdom of Robert Burns would sink its way to Kenneth's heart. The following sound was not that of words being exchanged by reasonable creatures. Kenneth did not retort as he always had. He made the noises of a wild alley cat, a starving alley cat. Edward's voice rang out in response. He did not quote a poet or philosopher, but hollered the sounds of a cornered beast.

"Run!" Edward shouted to Anika, "Run for your life!"

Anika turned from the cats and ran in the opposite direction. She ran into a wall, not one with a door to the alley beyond, but one with a tiny mouse hole. It was too tiny for a cat to follow, so she squeezed through the mouse hole to safety. There was not much beyond the hole, just a short and narrow space. She pressed against the end of it, praying that she was beyond the reach of a cat's arm.

Anika could not see what was happening. She dared not look. She obeyed Edward and kept herself pressed against a corner of the hole. She wept. Oh, she sobbed in fearful mourning. She pictured Edward at his best, strutting beside her, reciting Scottish literature, laughing as he rode the toboggan, squealing with delight as he popped from the tilting board. The sounds from outside the hole were horrible, the most violent and wild of cat fights. Only, it was not a cat fighting a cat, but four cats fighting a cat — four vicious cats fighting her dearest friend.

It did not sound like it was going well at all. Edward's voice had become intimately familiar to her, and it was only that voice that hollered out in pain. Anika's imagination allowed the sounds from outside of the hole to paint a vividly horrid picture in her mind. Oh, poor Edward. And poor Anika. What would become of her if Edward was killed?

The fighting went on and on, for hours, for days. As badly as Edward was hurt, he fought on in defense of his only friend. Just as despair wrapped its final finger around her throat, and sorrow held her lungs deflated, Anika felt a strange tingle across her entire body. Suddenly, she felt the top of the hole press against her head.

"I am growing!" she shouted, "The powder is fading and I am returning to me. But I am in this mouse hole. I do not fit in here."

She watched a single mouse claw turn to a human finger at the end of a growing mouse hand. Her neck bent awkwardly as she grew and pressed against the top, sides, and bottom of the mouse hole. She heard the cracking of the walls echo all around her, deep cracking that seemed to travel far in all directions. There was tremendous pressure on her, and she felt herself losing consciousness.

When she opened her eyes again, she was human. She was seated against a wall of the alley, covered in rubbish, in all the pieces of all the things that made up the Rubbish Manor. The alley was not dark, but lit by the sun above, as it was when they first drove into it.

"Ch...ch...child!" came the weak voice of the stuttering man from the university.

Anika gave him the briefest of glances before standing and looking frantically around her for her friend. There was no sign of Edward, no conniving Kenneth, no screeching, dancing, starving sisters. There was only a dirty alley, and a little man running toward her in a panic.

He stopped as he came to her, brushed some filth from her shoulders, and commented with disgust, "Child, you are covered in rubbish. What have you been doing? Have you been hiding from me?"

Anika wasn't sure how to answer. She managed only a stutter that was not unlike her driver's, "I-I-I..."

"Look, Anika," he came back more calming and compassionately, "I know you don't want to leave Edinburgh. B-But please, I must take you to your grandmother's farm. Maybe it won't be as bad as you imagine."

Anika looked around her one more time. There was no Rubbish Manor, no cats, no toboggan sleds, tilting boards, or boxes of toys, no booths of games and petit fours. And Anika — her trousers fit her perfectly, just as they did when she crawled into the car. It seemed like years ago, but maybe not.

79

"Just maybe," she thought to herself, "Just maybe it was a dream."

"It could not have been," she shouted, frightening the little man and sending him stumbling a few paces backward, "My heart has never hurt like this after a dream. I love him, and I miss him."

"Y... y... yes," the man remarked, "Of.., of course you miss your father. But soon you will be with family."

"I do miss my father," she said as a matter-of-fact, "But I wasn't talking about my father. I was talking about Edward, my cat friend with the bow tie and all the fancy quotations. We have to find him. I want to take from this alley, take him with me to the farm."

"You are talking nonsense, child," he replied with a chuckle as he took her by the hand.

He had to tug with all his might, but he led her to the car, which was not blocked by a skip bin. They drove easily out of the alley, out of Edinburgh, and northeast into the farm country northeast of Dundee. Anika's mind was a swirling storm of memories she tried to place in order. She held in her head what seemed like years of experiences in the Rubbish Manor. Before she could sort herself out, they were driving down the long driveway of her grandmother's farm.

The man's knock at the front door of the large farmhouse was as timid as his speech. It was plenty loud for the eager grandmother, who must have been waiting within a few paces on the other side. She swung the door wide and stood at the threshold. She was a large woman, with wide shoulders, a round face with happy wrinkles, and a broad smile with full, red lips.

"My sweet biscuit!" she shouted, as she took Anika's face in her hands and planted a substantial kiss on her forehead.

She turned to the driver and scolded, "I was expecting you hours ago. Where have you been?"

The nervous little man began a series of half-cooked excuses, none of which held the form of a completed sentence. Anika's grandmother invited them both in. Too embarrassed by the late arrival, too timid, too shy, who knows why, but the man declined the offer, mumbled some pleasantry or another, scurried like a mouse back to his car, and drove away.

With a slight, gentle push of the shoulders, Anika's grandmother escorted her to the living room couch.

"Some refreshments, of course," she announced to no particular audience, "I don't know what you have been about the last few hours, but you must be hungry."

Anika thought about it. She was still full, with the aftertaste of petit fours still in her mouth.

"I don't think it was a dream," she said directly to her grandmother.

"Did you have a dream, my dear? It is a long drive from Edinburgh, I have no doubt."

Anika went still and silent thinking about Edward, wondering where he went when the Rubbish Manor came down and how he fared in the vicious cat fight. She was snapped back to the moment by the ringing doorbell.

Her grandmother lumbered toward the front door, saying, "Wait here, my dear. This must be my young friend."

A boy accompanied her grandmother back to the living room. He was Anika's age, maybe a year older. He had red hair atop a soft, round face. His eyes — those familiar eyes. They were identical to those very eyes she had seen every day in the Rubbish Manor.

"Anika, this is my young friend, Edward. Your father used to read to me before he took you to the university. Now Edward reads to me. He is such a nice boy, smart, and cute too, wouldn't you say?"

He was a very cute boy, but he had a long scratch across his cheek.

"Oh my, what happened here?" the grandmother asked, pointing to the scratch and examining it closely.

Edward answered, "Kenneth scratched me again."

"Ohhh, that scoundrel of a cat. I would have tossed him out by now if I were your mother," the grandmother growled defensively.

"He is not a bad cat, just a little wild."

Anika stood from the couch and interrupted the moment, "Edward? Your name is Edward?"

"That is right," he answered, "And you are Anika. I have heard much about you."

Anika's grandmother forgot that it was Edward's day to come read to her, and she tried to apologize to the boy, "Oh Edward, I am so sorry. But Anika has just arrived. Maybe you can come over in a few days."

"No, no," Anika interrupted, "Please don't send him out on my account. I would like to hear him read to you, just as my father used to."

"Very well," the grandmother returned.

She sat in her chair across from the couch. Edward sat on the other side of the couch, opposite of Anika. He took a book from the side table and opened it. He began, "To a Mouse, On Turning Her Up in Her Nest with the Plough, by Robert Burns, November 1785,"

Small, crafty, cowering, timorous little

beast,

O, what a panic is in your little breast!

You need not start away so hasty

With argumentative chatter!

I would be loath to run and chase you,

With murdering plough-staff

Anika's grandmother sat up to the edge of her chair and asked Edward, "What are you doing? Those aren't the words. Why are you reading it that way?"

"Being a sensible boy," Edward answered, "being a gentile boy, one with manners, I speak so that all around me can understand."

The grandmother looked to Anika, nodded, turned back to Edward, and said, "Very well, but it is much better as Burns wrote it, in Scots."

Edward continued where he left off, translating on the spot,

I'm truly sorry man's dominion

Has broken Nature's social union,

And justifies that ill opinion

Which makes you startle

At me, your poor, earth born companion

And fellow mortal!

While the very familiar voice, behind the very familiar eyes, recited Burns, Anika warmed from her inside out. With a widening smile, she watched and listened while Edward translated the third stanza. When he began the fourth, she silently mouthed the first line, thinking about the Rubbish Manor,

Your small house, too, in ruin!

Its feeble walls the winds are scattering!

And nothing now, to build a new one,

Of coarse green foliage!

And bleak December's winds coming,

Both bitter and piercing!

Before he began the fifth stanza, Anika stood suddenly and quickly, and held up her hand. Edward silenced, as he and the grandmother both stared at her.

Her grandmother asked her, "Are you well, my dear?"

Edward followed with, "Should I continue?"

"No Edward," Anika answered, "It is my turn. This one is mine."

With no book in hand and no need for translations among her company, she recited,

Thy wee bit heap o' leaves an' stibble,

Has cost thee mony a weary nibble!

Now thou's turn'd out, for a' thy trouble,

But house or hald,

To thole the winter's sleety dribble,

An' cranreuch cauld!

But, Mousie, thou art no thy-lane,

In proving foresight may be vain;

The best-laid schemes o' mice an' men

Gang aft agley,

An' lea'e us nought but grief an' pain,

For promis'd joy!

Still thou art blest, compar'd wi' me

The present only toucheth thee:

But, Och! I backward cast my e'e.

On prospects drear!

An' forward, tho' I canna see,

I guess an' fear!

The End

Dedication

This story is dedicated to Robert Burns,
Allan Ramsay, and Walter Scott,
to Gershom Carmichael and David Hume,
and the many great Scottish scribblers
whose words and wisdom
have brought beauty and clarity to this
confusing world.